This Little Tiger book belongs to:

_____

_____

_____

For three-legged dogs everywhere ~ J K

For every one of my pets, past, present and future.
Each of you so very loved, each of you so very perfect ~ S L

LITTLE TIGER PRESS LTD,
an imprint of the Little Tiger Group
1 Coda Studios, 189 Munster Road, London SW6 6AW
www.littletiger.co.uk

First published in Great Britain 2018
This edition published 2019

Text copyright © John Kelly 2018
Illustrations copyright © Steph Laberis 2018

John Kelly and Steph Laberis have asserted their rights to be identified as the author and illustrator
of this work under the Copyright, Designs and Patents Act, 1988

A CIP catalogue record for this book is available from the British Library

All rights reserved • ISBN 978-1-84869-950-2

Printed in China • LTP/2700/2574/1118

2 4 6 8 10 9 7 5 3 1

What Do You Do if Your House is a Zoo?

John Kelly   Steph Laberis

LITTLE TIGER
LONDON

On Sunday, Mum and Dad said,
"You can have a pet!"

Hurrah!
At last!

But what pet did I want? I just couldn't decide.

So on Monday, I put an advert in the local paper.

LITTLE BUMBLING NEWS

· CLASSIFIEDS ·

IN SEARCH OF . . .

Cave too stinky?
Friends won't stop
snoring?
Then get away from
it all at . . .
The Hibernation
Hotel

Could you be the
pet for me?
If so, contact me, Oscar, at:
99 Ice Cream Drive,
Little Bumbling

Looking for friends?
Join 'Our Cl...
Anyone wel...
No joining...

FOR SALE

For Sale!
(One careful owner)
• Emperor Flabulon video game
• The Windy Pirates DVD
• Penguin All-Stars sticker book

Rare!
"Hiss" Autographed LP.
Signed by all the band
...st on to
...details

And on Tuesday . . .

. . . I got some replies!

The first one was on **VERY** fancy paper.

To whom it may concern,

You may address me as 'Your Highness' or by my full title, Princess Cushion-Slasher Furball the Third.

If I am to grace your dwelling with my royal bottom, I shall require the following:

1. Lots of cushions or laps.

2. No other pets, especially dogs. (Goldfish are acceptable.)

3. My own 24-hour private entrance.

4. Fresh fish. Fresh cream. Fresh chicken. No tins!

Yours sincerely,

Princess

The next was **short** and **sweet** (but a little bit damp).

Hi! My name is Goldie!
I don't eat very much and I live
in a nice clean bowl . . .
Hi! My name is Goldie!
I don't eat very much and I—
OOH!, LOOK!
        A treasure chest!
Goldie x x x

And the last one had been **nibbled**

by the sender!

MY NAME IS BiLL. BiLLY G. GRUFF.
AND BY MY BEARD i AIN'T FUSSY.
I'LL EAT ANYTHING.
GRASS, FLOWERS, HATS
YRES, CuPS, CHAIRS,
CHAIR   Y LiNERS,   OTBA
        'E,   ATS,
            CHEESE, POTATO PEELINGS,

This was going to be tough.
And it got even tougher, because on
Wednesday the postman brought more replies.

LOADS MORE!

And the more I read . . .

From: J. BROWNPAWS

OSCAR
99 ICE CREAM DR
LITTLE BUMBLING

From: Dash G.

OSCAR
99 ICE CREAM DR
Little Bumbling

From: T. Tiger

From: P. Woofers

OSCAR
99 ICE C

. . . the more confused I got!

There were so many animals,
the choice was making me **DIZZY!**

We're the meerkats! We'll keep you safe!

We'll PROTECT you from EVERYTHING.

Security guaranteed—
24 hours a day!

Greetings, tiny adorable human!
You're such a cutie!
I just want to pick you up,
cuddle you, and climb to the top
of the Empire State Building.
YOU will be the
perfect pet for me!

Hi! My name is Olive.
We could go for a nice long run
together and get away from everything.
Or we could just stick our heads
in the sand. I don't mind, really.
Please pick me! Olive xx

Greetings! I am Anthony.
This is my brother, Anthony, my other brother, Anthony,
and my 12,359 other brothers called Anthony. We live with my mum,
Queenie, but are quickly running out of space. Can we com
and live with you? We're neat and tidy
and great at heavy lifting. xx

Heigh-ho! Henrietta here!
You sound like a WINNER!
I'm a winner too!
Best in show
(three years in a row).
• Highest jumper
• Shiniest coat • Smartest hooves
I'd love to be your pet (as long as you always let me win).

Space Monkey
Boo-Boo calling!
I'm looking for a place
to crash and somewhere
test my new rocket.*
I blast off in search of
the banana planet next
Tuesday, and I can't wait
to be your pet!

*It's not dangerous at all.
It probably won't even blow
up this time.

WILF THE WOLF HERE.
I MAY BE LONG IN THE TOOTH
(AND A LITTLE BIT GREY) BUT I CAN
STILL KEEP UP WITH THE PACK.

I MIGHT NEED A BIT OF A LIE DOWN
AFTERWARDS, THOUGH.

BILL &
BOB BEAVER

We're not just pets.
We're builders* extraordinaire!
No job too big.
Experts in gardening.
Water features a speciality!

*Looking for new
premises due to
unexpected flooding.

Name's Ollie. Jolly busy! Can't wait to be your pet!
Likes: Juggling, ping-pong, filing, washing up, knitting.
Dislikes: Sitting still.
Bye-bye!

SNORT!

Bertram's the name.
China's the game!
I need somewhere to display my rather
delicate collection of precious antique
bone china.

Bertram.

Why would Walter Whale (me)
make a wonderful pet?
Well, whales are no trouble at all.
All we need is a small lake, river, or Olympic-
sized swimming pool, and five tonnes of shrimp
every day (four as I'm currently on a diet).
Wettest wishes, Walter xx

And to make matters worse, on Thursday
the meerkats arrived. They set up a security post
and wouldn't let Mum leave!

"I'll be late for work!" she cried until . . .

. . . Kingsley the gorilla kindly gave her a lift.

"That looks like fun!" I cried. "Can I go too?"

"**No way!**" said Dad. "Why on earth did you invite them?"

"I didn't!" I started to explain,

but before I could finish . . .

. . . the Beaver Brothers appeared and built us a **LOVELY** water feature. This was more like it! I yelled, **"Geronimo!"** and was about to dive in when . . .

Walter Whale swam up
and turned Mr and Mrs Jones'
barbecue into a pool party!

"Right!" said Dad as he blow-dried Mr Jones' wig.

"No more animals!"

INVOICE

But they kept on coming – our house felt like a zoo!
Soon I was surrounded by pets, but not one
of them wanted to play with me.

In fact, our house was so full
we ended up sleeping
in the garden.
"Peace at last,"
sighed Dad when,

WHOOSH!
CrUNCh!
TINKLE!

we were woken by
Space Monkey Boo-Boo
crash-landing on the
potting shed.

"THAT'S IT!"
cried Mum.
"They've ALL got to go!"

I was sad to see the animals leave.

But I don't think any of them was the pet for me.

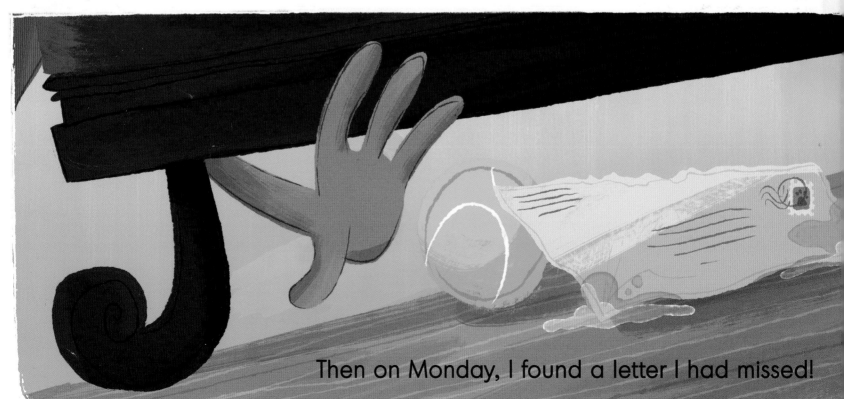

Then on Monday, I found a letter I had missed!

It was **whiffy, drooly,** and covered in **stray hairs,**
but I opened it anyway.

Pick me!
I love you!
We've never met, but
I love you already!

My name is Rufus,
but I answer to: **BAD DOG!**
STOP THAT! and **GET**
OFF THAT CHAIR!

I like running (a lot),
and jumping, and rolling,
and balls, and mud, and chasing
cats, and running!
I'm very loyal and we'll be
best friends **FOREVER.**
Rufus xxx

P.S. I'll eat anything, but I would much rather eat your food.

And suddenly I realised that the pet for me isn't
the one that **I WANT** . . .

. . . it's THE ONE THAT WANTS ME!